This book ~~book~~ fart belongs to

CALLUM

FROM
GRANDPA

make believe ideas ltd

The Wilderness, Berkhamsted, Hertfordshire, HP4 2AZ, UK.
501 Nelson Place, P.O. Box 141000, Nashville, TN 37214-1000, USA.

www.makebelieveideas.com

Written by Franklin P. Hartie.
Illustrated by Lara Ede.

FRANK the FART fairy

Written by Franklin P. Hartie • Illustrated by Lara Ede

make believe ideas

Fairies were one of three magical creatures that never **farted.**

Mermaids were another who never **broke wind** (they didn't have bottoms so they couldn't),

and yetis were too embarrassed to **bottom burp** ... or even normal burp!

CAN'T FART

WON'T FART

Gnomes, on the other hand, couldn't stop **farting**
and were only second on the **FART-O-METER**
of fartiness to one other creature . . .

SECRET
SQUEAKER

REGULAR
RIP-TICKLER

EXPLOSIVE
ERUPTIONS

...HUMANS.

And with most things that humans lost, hid, and left behind ... the fairies were on the case.

Well, one fairy was. His name was **FRANK the FART FAIRY.**

THE HUMAN

FARTS: 15 times a day...500,000 farts a lifetime!

FART FACT:

The word "human", which comes from an old fairy language, means "stink butt".

It was Frank's job to stop all the **gassy bottom pops.**

All those **silent stinkers** that wafted across the room.

The many **bubble-and-squeaks** that turned baths into Jacuzzis.

He was even there on those rare occasions when your mom **let one rip!**

However, the farts Frank trapped didn't always stay trapped for long.

That's because, as well as finding **farts** hilarious, Frank also used them to **prank.**

He loved to **bubble prank** the mermaids at the Sunset Lagoon . . .

"It wasn't me!"

"Don't pop them!"

"They tickle!"

. . . **stink bomb** the flower fairies in Rainbow Meadow . . .

"Avalanche!"

. . . and let off **fart explosions** on Mount Yeti!

However, one day, Frank went one **fart prank** too far.

"The agenda for today's meeting is this year's Fairy-Con…" **FARRRRRRRRT!**

And it **backfired!**

The fairies, the mermaids, the yetis, and even the gnomes had had enough of Frank's **farty** antics.

"Farts are NOT funny," lectured the Fairy Godmother. "Neither are pranks, wisecracks, or jokes about farts!"

"But... **but...**"

"Butts are also not funny. You are banned from Fairy Land!"

Frank couldn't believe it.

He was going to **miss** his favorite, number-one event in the fairy calendar: Fairy-Con,

where fairies could show off their talents and maybe get an autograph or two!

"It's not fairy fair!" moaned Frank.
"My farts are funny, my pranks
are hilarious, and my jokes about
farts are hysterical.
I'll show them!"

Even though Frank was in a LOT of trouble, he decided the best thing to do was plan the ultimate **FART PRANK** ... and where better to play that prank than at Fairy-Con!

Frank set to work, vacuuming up the most **fierce farts,** the most **bubbly bottom burps,** and the stinkiest stink bombs.

He then trapped each **fart** in a mini cushion.

"I think I will call my new invention a . . .
FARTY PILLOW!"

Soon the big day arrived! Frank disguised himself as a
superhero fairy and crept into the bustling Fairy-Con.

He went from chair to chair . . .

. . . sofa to sofa . . .

. . . fairy toilet to fairy toilet (yes, there are such things) . . .

. . . and hid hundreds of fart-filled farty pillows.

What happened next became known in fairy folklore as . . .

...the Epic Farty-works Display!

It started with a gnome... **PARP!**

Then a couple of fairies... **FRARPP!**

Then the Tooth Fairy... **BRRPPP!**

Suddenly, the whole of Fairy-Con was filled with the sounds and smells
of hundreds of farty pillows being sat on!

FART!

FART!

FART!

FART!

FART!

FART!

FART!

FART!

But that wasn't what made the Fairy Godmother turn purple with anger.

It was what happened next.

For the **first** time in fairy history, a fairy **farted** ... for real!

The sounds of the farty pillows had caused a gassy chain reaction.

The fairies couldn't help it.

One after another, they **broke wind** ...

... **Let rip** ...

... and **squeaked** one out!

But unlike gross human farts, fairy **farts** sounded like melodic harps, smelled of real raspberries, and were made of … magic!

And all the magical fairy farts exploded in a cascade of glorious glitter that fell all over Frank.

As the fairy farts settled, everyone peeked out from where they were hiding. And there, in the spot where Frank was last seen, was a large, ginger-haired **farty pillow** that looked a LOT like a prank-loving Fart Fairy.

Everyone started to laugh, even the Fairy Godmother.

Frank didn't understand.

"Why is everyone laughing at me?"

Frank turned and saw himself on the large, Fairy-Con TV screen.

"I've... (parp!) ... **turned into** ... (brrrp!) ... **a giant farty pillow!**"

"That's enough fun for one Fairy-Con," said the Fairy Godmother.

And with a swish of her wand, Frank was back to normal.

"I'm sorry," said Frank.

"Frank, all farts aren't always funny," said the Fairy Godmother. "Some jokes are sometimes funny, and a prank is only funny if it's not played on you."

T-SHIRT

FRANK 'N' FARTER

Frank learned a very important lesson, and from that day on he vowed never to prank a fairy, a mermaid, a yeti, or a gnome ever again.

Instead, he set up his own farty pillow factory so everyone else could prank each other!

(Frank later changed the name to **WHOOPEE** cushions.

For some reason, the name "farty pillows" didn't catch on!)

THE END